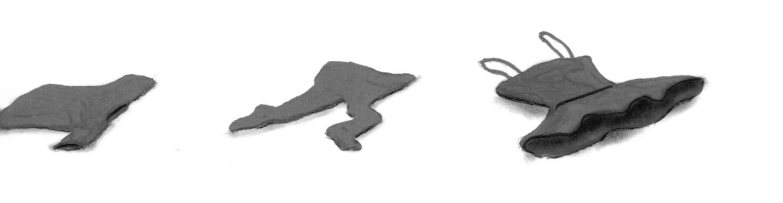

OLIVIA

written and illustrated by Ian Falconer

SIMON AND SCHUSTER

First published in Great Britain in 2000 by Simon and Schuster
1st Floor, 222 Gray's Inn Road, London WC1X 8HB
A CBS Company
This paperback edition first published 2004

Originally published in 2000 by Atheneum Books for Young Readers,
an imprint of Simon & Schuster Children's Publishing Division, New York
Copyright © 2000 Ian Falconer

Book design by Ann Bobco
The text of this book is set in Centaur
The illustrations are rendered in charcoal and gouache on paper

Printed in Italy

A CIP catalogue reference for this book is available from the British Library

ISBN: 978 0 68986 088 I
10

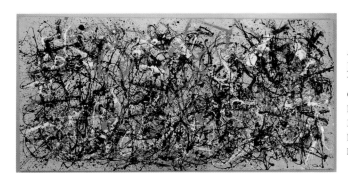

A detail from *Autumn Rhythm #30* by Jackson Pollock appears on page 29. The Metropolitan Museum of Art, George A. Hearn Fund, 1957. (57.92) Photograph © 1998 The Metropolitan Museum of Art. Used courtesy of the Pollock-Krasner Foundation/Artists Rights Society (ARS), New York.

A detail from *Ballet Rehearsal on the Set*, 1874, by Edgar Degas, appears on page 26. Oil on canvas, 2′ 1½″ x 2′ 8″ (65 x 81 cm), used courtesy of the Musée d'Orsay, Paris.

To the real Olivia and Ian,
and to William,
who didn't arrive in time to appear in this book.

This is Olivia.

She is good at lots of things.

She is *very* good at wearing people out.

She even wears herself out.

Olivia has a little brother named Ian.
He's always copying.

Sometimes Ian just won't leave her alone,
so Olivia has to be firm.

Olivia lives with her mother, her father, her brother,
her dog, Perry,

and Edwin, the cat.

In the morning, after she gets up,
and moves the cat,

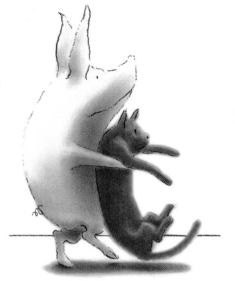

and brushes her teeth,
and combs her ears,

and moves the cat,

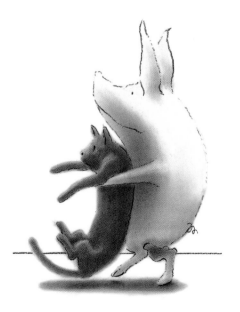

  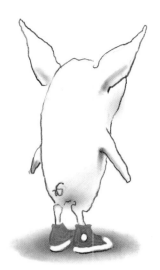

Olivia gets dressed.

She has to try on
everything.

On sunny days, Olivia likes to go to the beach.

She feels it's important
to come prepared.

Last summer when Olivia was little,
her mother showed her how to make sandcastles.

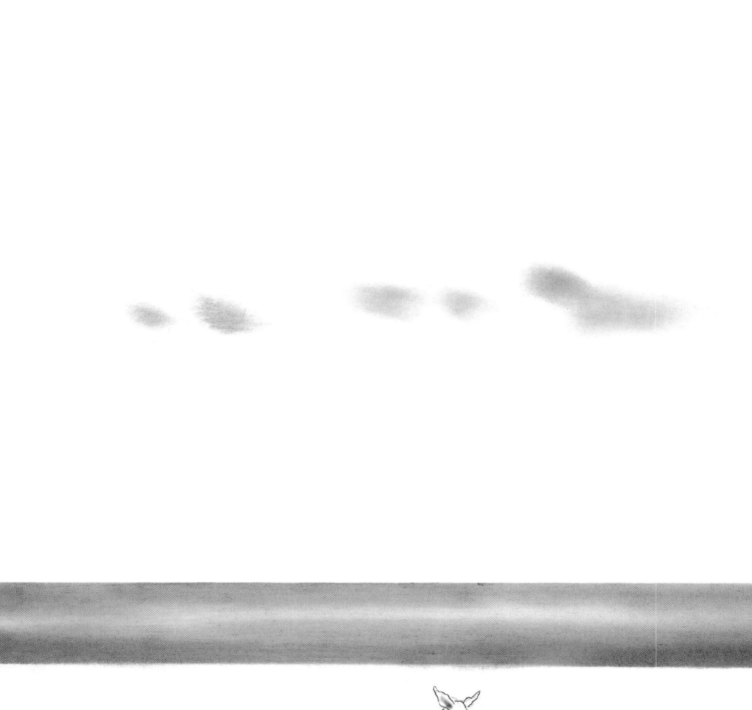

She got pretty good.

Sometimes Olivia
likes to bask in
the sun.

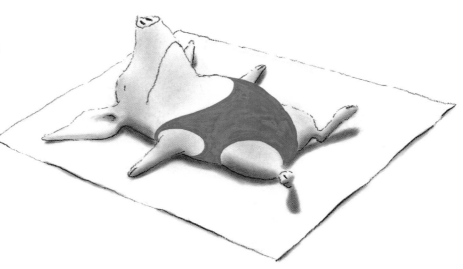

When her mother sees that she's had enough,
they go home.

Every day Olivia is supposed to take a nap.
"It's time for your you-know-what," her mother says.

Of course Olivia's not at all sleepy.

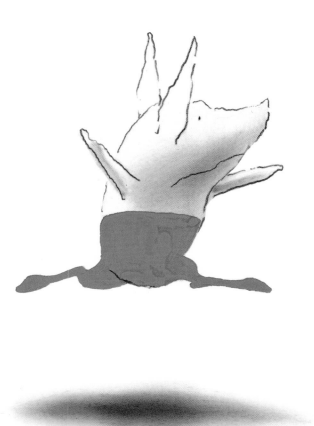

On rainy days, Olivia likes to go to the museum.

She heads straight for her favourite picture.

Olivia looks at it for a long time.
What could she be thinking?

But there is one painting Olivia just doesn't get.
"I could do that in about five minutes," she says to her mother.

As soon as she gets home she gives it a try.

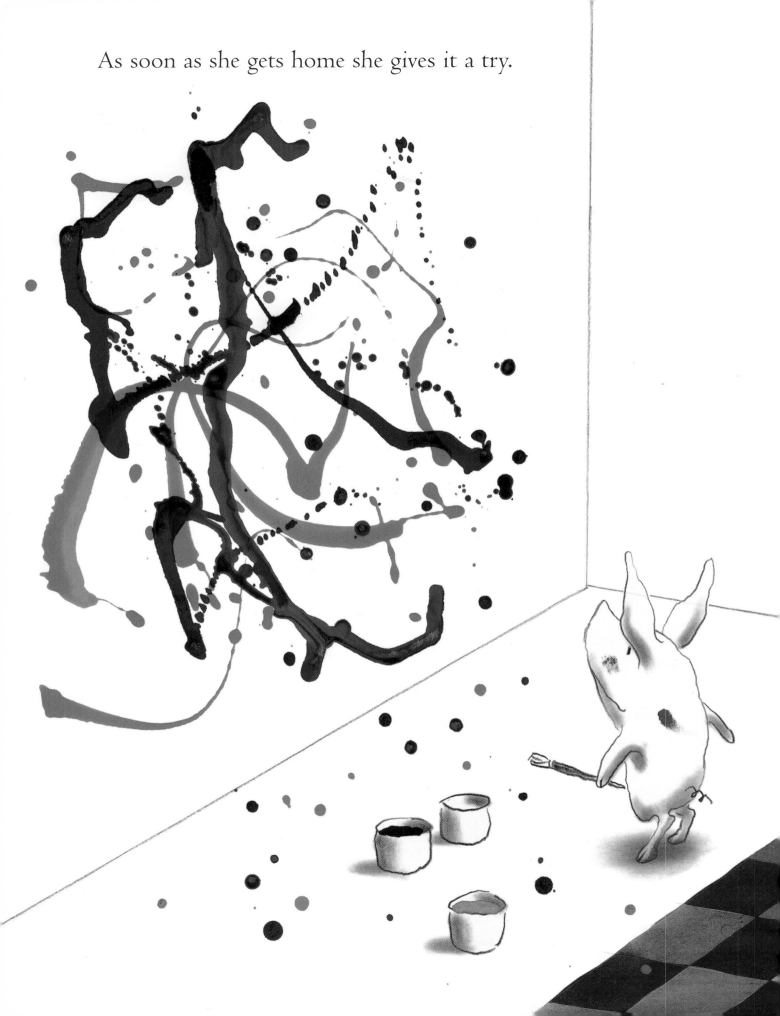

Time out.

After a nice bath,

and a nice dinner,

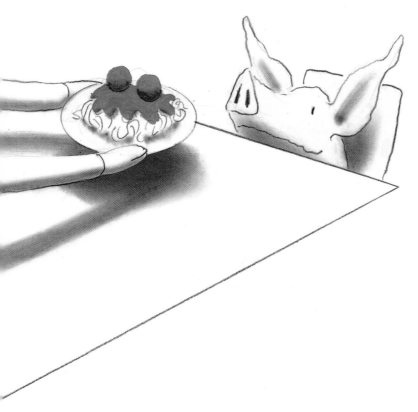

it's time for bed.

But of course Olivia's not at all sleepy.

"Only five books tonight, Mummy," she says.

"No, Olivia, just one."
"How about four?"
"Two."
"Three."
"Oh, all right, three.
    But that's *it!*"

When they've finished reading, Olivia's mother gives her
a kiss and says, "You know, you really wear me out.
But I love you anyway."
And Olivia gives her a kiss back and says,
"I love you anyway too."